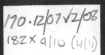

# DAD'S DINOSAUR DAY

# DIANE DAWSON HEARN

# DAD'S
# DINOSAUR
# DAY

MACMILLAN PUBLISHING COMPANY   NEW YORK
MAXWELL MACMILLAN CANADA   TORONTO
MAXWELL MACMILLAN INTERNATIONAL
NEW YORK   OXFORD   SINGAPORE   SYDNEY

First edition
Printed in the United States of America

10  9  8  7  6  5  4  3  2  1

The text of this book is set in 18 pt. Zapf International Light.
The illustrations are rendered in pen and ink and watercolor.

Library of Congress Cataloging-in-Publication Data
Hearn, Diane Dawson. Dad's dinosaur day / Diane Dawson Hearn. — 1st ed.    p.    cm. Summary: Dad's behavior changes when he becomes a dinosaur for a day. ISBN 0-02-743485-0  [1. Fathers—Fiction.  2. Dinosaurs—Fiction.] I. Title. PZ7.H3455Dad 1993    [E]—dc20    92-22549

In loving memory of
ERIC W. HEARN

At breakfast yesterday, Dad wasn't himself at all.

"What happened to Dad?" I shouted.

"I guess he's having a dinosaur day, Mikey," said Mom.

"Aren't you going to go to work?" I asked him.
"Dinosaurs don't know how to work," roared Dad.

"Aren't you going to drive me to school?"
"Dinosaurs don't know how to drive," roared Dad.

So I rode to school a different way.

Dad stayed and helped out on the playground.

At lunch the kids shared their food with him.
He liked the salad best.

After school all my friends begged to come with us,
but they had to ride the bus.

We took the long way home so Dad could have a snack.

"You're both a mess!" cried Mom
when we got to our house.
"Take a bath right now."
"Dinosaurs don't fit into bathtubs," roared Dad.

So we took a shower.

That night we ate in the yard.
Dad had his pizza with everything on it.

"Time for Mikey's stories," said Mom after dinner.
"Dinosaurs don't know how to read," roared Dad.
So I read my books to him.

When it was time for bed,
Dad was too sleepy to tuck me in.
So I tucked him in.

"I'm glad Dad had fun today," I told Mom.
"But I'd like to get my old dad back."
"Oh, I'm sure you will," said Mom,
kissing me good-night.

When I came down to breakfast today,
Dad was himself again.
"Breakfast isn't ready yet," he said.
"Do you know where your mother is?"

"Dinosaurs don't know how to cook," roared Mom.